Curly the Piglet

Curly the Piglet

by
Cynthia Overbeck

CAROLRHODA BOOKS
MINNEAPOLIS, MINNESOTA U.S.A.

Revised English text by Cynthia Overbeck. Original French text by Anne-Marie Pajot. Translation by Dyan Hammarberg. Photographs by Guy Dhuit. Drawings by L'Enc Matte.

LIBRARY OF CONGRESS CATALOGING IN PUBLICATION DATA

Overbeck, Cynthia
Curly, the piglet.

(The Animal Friends Books)
Original ed. published under title: Basile, le porcelet.
SUMMARY: Two farm children are concerned about the runt in the new litter of piglets and decide to take care of it themselves.

1. Swine—Juvenile literature. 2. Animals, Infancy of—Juvenile literature. 3. Farm life—Juvenile literature. [1. Pigs. 2. Farm life] I. Pajot, Anne Marie. Basile, le porcelet. II. Dhuit, Guy. III. Matte, L'Enc. IV. Title.

SF395.5.O85 1976   636.4   76-3431
ISBN 0-87614-069-X

First published in the United States of America 1976 by Carolrhoda Books, Inc. All English language rights reserved.

Original edition published by Librairie A. Hatier, Paris, France, under the title BASILE LE PORCELET.
English text and drawings © 1976 Carolrhoda Books, Inc.
Photographs © 1969 Librairie A. Hatier.

Manufactured in the United States of America.
Published simultaneously in Canada by J. M. Dent & Sons (Canada) Ltd., Don Mills, Ontario.

International Standard Book Number: 0-87614-069-X
Library of Congress Catalog Card Number: 76-3431

Susie and Mark live on a large farm where their parents raise pigs and corn. For the children, springtime on the farm is always the most exciting season of the year. It is the time when many of the farm animals' babies are born.

This spring, Mark and Susie are especially excited. A few days ago, one of the pigs on the farm gave birth to a large litter of 11 baby pigs!

Mark and Susie are eager to see the piglets, so they get up early one morning and hurry down to the trough. There they find the mother pig, who is taking her new babies for an outing.

Next to their enormous mother, the piglets look so small and lively! But one looks smaller than the rest—so small that Mark and Susie wonder if he will ever grow up. Because he is the "runt" of the litter, the children feel sorry for him. They name him Curly, and they decide to make him their special pet.

Susie and Mark kneel by the fence to get a closer look at Curly and the other piglets. The little creatures are bright pink, with curly tails and floppy ears. On each of their feet are four toes—two little toes, and two big front toes covered by hard "toenails," called *hooves*.

In a few days, the piglets' body hair will begin to grow stiff and bristly. Right now, though, it is as smooth as velvet. Like their mother, the piglets have small eyes and cannot see very well. But they have a good sense of smell. They sniff along the ground, using their snouts, or noses, to explore their farmyard home.

The mother pig, called a *sow*, is busy eating from the feed trough. She weighs nearly 440 pounds (200 kilograms). That's heavier than Mark, Susie, and their parents put together!

Right now, the piglets are much, much smaller than their mother. But they will grow quickly. They have such big appetites that they eat a meal every two hours.

In fact, it's suppertime for the piglets right now. The sow lies down on her side, and the piglets push and squeeze to get a taste of their mother's good, warm milk. The sow has 12 nipples. Each piglet chooses one of them and always sucks milk from the same nipple.

The piglets are enjoying their meal. But Mark and Susie are worried, because Curly is not there. Even though there is a nipple for him, he is too small to push his way in through the squirming group of piglets.

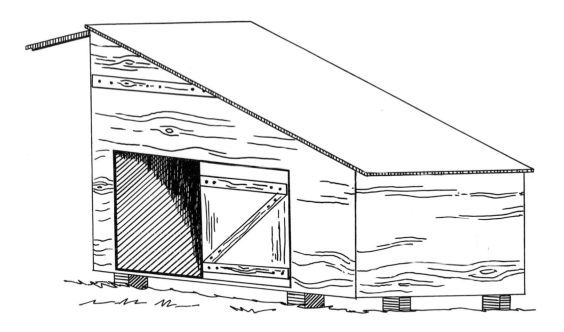

The children love Curly, and they are sad to see him left out. Because he is so small, he cannot join in the rough-and-tumble games that the other piglets play. His brothers and sisters love to jump and roll about in the straw all day long. But Curly would rather trot along behind Mark and avoid being bumped around.

When night comes, the piglets are tired out after a long day of romping and exploring. They fall asleep in a heap, pressed close together. The piglets sleep in a special pig shed, on a bed of clean, dry straw. They like a tidy place to sleep, because they are naturally very clean animals—not dirty, as most people think.

Curly is tired, too, but he does not join his brothers and sisters. So Mark carries him to the pig house himself and puts him in the straw next to the other piglets for warmth.

The next morning, the piglets go out into the farmyard for another day of play. But Curly hangs back. He has hardly eaten at all, and he is beginning to look thin and weak. Mark and Susie are worried.

"What shall we do?" asks Mark. "We've got to make Curly eat, or he may die."

"I have an idea," says Susie. "If he won't drink his mother's milk, we'll feed him ourselves. We'll give him a bottle, like a human baby!"

The children fix a bottle of warm milk for Curly. But the first time they try to feed him, he doesn't like the bottle at all. He trembles and wriggles, and he finally slips out of Mark's arms just as a few drops of good milk fall on his tongue.

But Susie and Mark keep trying. Soon Curly is so eager to drink the milk that he comes running when he sees the children with the bottle. He sits happily in Mark's lap while Susie feeds him.

In a few days, Curly begins to gain weight. He starts to run and play in the farmyard with the other piglets.

Now that the piglets are about three weeks old, they are ready to be weaned from their mother. This means that they will gradually learn to eat solid food instead of drinking their mother's milk. When pigs are allowed to run free in the woods, they eat chestnuts, roots, and acorns. But on the farm they eat mash, a food made of oats, corn, or barley mixed with skim milk or water. The pigs also like crushed potatoes and kitchen scraps. They have such an appetite that they'll eat just about anything.

Because Susie and Mark have taken such good care of Curly, he is beginning to look strong and healthy. By the time he's six months old, he'll weigh more than 200 pounds (90 kilograms). He has already grown so big that Mark can hardly hold him in his arms. Susie and Mark decide that it's time for Curly to be on his own.

"It makes me sad to let Curly go," Mark says to his sister.

"Me too," she replies. "But I'm glad that we helped to make him so healthy. And Dad is proud of us. He tells everyone what we've done."

As a matter of fact, their father is so pleased that he promises to take Curly to the farm show someday. All the farmers take their best animals to the show. There are prizes for the cow that gives the most milk, for the sheep with the thickest wool, *and* for the fattest pig.

"Eat a lot of mash, Curly," the children call to their pet. "We worked hard for you. Maybe someday you'll win us a blue ribbon!"

DO YOU KNOW ...

- why pigs wallow in the mud?

- how many teeth pigs have?

- what we use pig bristles for?

TO FIND THE ANSWERS TO THESE QUESTIONS,
TURN THE PAGE 👉

FACTS ABOUT PIGS

Hogs, or pigs, belong to the group of mammals—warm-blooded animals that nurse their babies.

Male pigs are called *boars*; females are called *sows*. All newborn baby pigs are called *piglets*.

Pigs are *omnivorous* (ahm-NIV-er-us)—that is, they eat both meat and plants. Most farm pigs eat mash, a mixture of milk or water and grain. Corn is the grain that makes the best pig food. More than half of the corn grown in the United States is used to feed pigs.

There are many breeds, or kinds, of farm pigs. Some of the most common breeds are shown below.

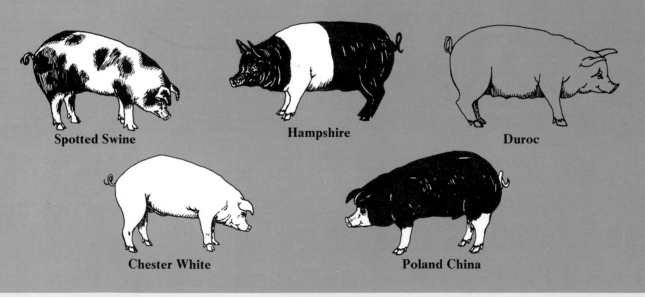

Spotted Swine

Hampshire

Duroc

Chester White

Poland China

People use farm pigs for food. The stiff shiny hairs, or *bristles*, that grow on the pigs' skins are used to make hairbrushes. And the skins themselves are made into fine pigskin leather.

All pigs have 44 teeth. Adult males often have two sharp tusks, which they use as digging tools and as weapons. Because these tusks can be dangerous, farmers usually clip them off.

A pig's nose is called a *snout*. In farm pigs, the snout may be either long and narrow, or short and broad.

Pigs have four hooved toes on each foot. The large hooves that cover the two front toes look almost like one hoof that has been cloven, or split.

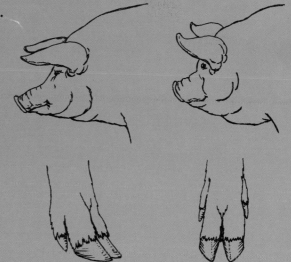

Pigs are very clean, intelligent creatures. Because they like to wallow in mud, people think that they are dirty animals. But pigs must lie in mud or water on hot days because they do not have any sweat glands to help them cool off.

The farm pig has several wild relatives, including the *wild boar*, which lives in southwest and central Asia and in North Africa, and the *wart hog*, a strange-looking inhabitant of the southern African plains.

Wild Boar

Wart Hog

The Animal Friends Books

Clover the CALF
Jessie the CHICKEN
Ali the DESERT FOX
Splash the DOLPHIN
Dolly the DONKEY
Downy the DUCKLING
ELEPHANTS around the World
Tippy the FOX TERRIER
Marigold the GOLDFISH
Polly the GUINEA PIG
Winslow the HAMSTER
Figaro the HORSE

Rusty the IRISH SETTER
Boots the KITTEN
Penny and Pete the LAMBS
The LIONS of Africa
Mandy the MONKEY
Lorito the PARROT
Curly the PIGLET
Whiskers the RABBIT
Shelley the SEA GULL
Penelope the TORTOISE
Sprig the TREE FROG
Tanya the TURTLE DOVE

CAROLRHODA BOOKS
241 FIRST AVENUE NORTH – MINNEAPOLIS, MINNESOTA 55401

*Published in memory of Carolrhoda Locketz Rozell,
Who loved to bring children and books together*

Please write for a complete catalogue